Twinkle Friend

Twinkle, twinkle little me,

2

I'm as special as can be.

3

There's no one quite like me, it's true,

and my friends are special, too.

Twinkle, twinkle little me,

I'm as special as can be.

Twinkle, twinkle, little star,

what a special friend you are.

From your head to your toes,

we are special friends, you know.

Twinkle, twinkle, little star,
what a special friend you are.